THE SPINJITZU SAGAS

ISBN 978-0-545-81672-4

10 9 8 7 6 5 4 3   18 19 20 21 22
Printed in China   38

First printing 2017

SCHOLASTIC INC.

A SECRET MISSION

"Things are looking up," Cole said. He and the other ninja were on Master Chen's island for the Tournament of Elements. They had come to find their friend Zane, who was a prisoner. When Cole lost his tournament battle, he became Chen's prisoner, too.

"We came here to find a friend," Cole told Karlof, another elemental fighter. "I found him. All I gotta do is get Zane and get outta here!"

"But it's impossible to escape this place," said Karlof. The two new friends were stuck working in Master Chen's fortune cookie factory.

Cole shrugged. "I'm working out the details. But first, I gotta let the other ninja know I'm bustin' Zane out." He held up a tiny slip of paper.

"You put a message in a cookie?" Karlof gasped. "I hope you have the good fortune for it to end up in the right hands."

Upstairs in the palace, Master Chen was hosting a banquet. "Let's celebrate the eight contestants who made it to the second round!" he cheered.

But the ninja didn't trust Master Chen. They knew he was trying to steal everyone's powers. Jay, Kai, and Lloyd had formed a secret alliance with the other Elemental Masters—everyone but Shade, Master of Shadow.

"If you plan to stop Chen," Garmadon told the ninja, "you'll need everyone on board."

Clouse leaned toward Chen. "Our guests have allied themselves."

"Do they know about the spell?" Chen hissed.

Clouse shook his head. "Not yet."

Chen stood up. "I know there are rumors that I am stealing everyone's powers . . . I am," he announced.

Everyone gasped.

"But it's all for this staff!" Chen continued.

"The staff holds the powers of your fallen foes," Chen said. "The last person standing in my tournament will win it!"

"What about the spell?" Lloyd asked.

"Spell? What spell?" Clouse asked.

"Don't believe him," Lloyd told the others. "It's a trick!"

"Why should we believe you, Lloyd?" asked Shade.

Clouse chuckled. "The alliance is crumbling. Very clever, Master."

"We need to find that spell," Jay whispered. He turned to a Kabuki dancer who kept whacking him with her fan. "Cut it out!"

"Jay, it's me—Nya," the dancer whispered. "I'm undercover."

Kai grinned. "Then you can get close to Clouse's spell book!"

Nya nodded. "I'll look into it. But you need to look into something, too. *You* have a spy!"

Skylor, Master of Amber, cracked open
her fortune cookie. "Look! Cole and Zane are
breaking out. You're lucky this message didn't
end up in the wrong hands."

"Cole found Zane! I can't believe it," Kai
cried. "Thanks, Skylor. It's good to know there
are some people here we can trust."

"Who do you think the spy is?" Jay asked.

Lloyd stared at Shade. "I have my suspicions."

Nya hurried away to call Dareth, who'd helped her sneak on to the island. "Dareth, are you there?"

The Brown Ninja answered from Nya's hidden mobile unit. "Loud and proud, Nya. Talk to me."

"I'm going to find the spell while the ninja sniff out a spy," Nya told him.

"Aye aye, Samurai X," agreed Dareth. "Brown Ninja out."

THE ESCAPE PLAN

Back at the factory, Cole was working on his escape plan. He needed to steal the guards' keys. He distracted them by grabbing some noodles.

"Don't touch the merchandise!" a guard hollered. "Get him!"

"Let there be food!" Cole cried, gobbling a handful of cookies. "Now I'm runnin' on cookie power!"

Cole used a long string of noodles to swing himself over the guards. "Woo-hoo!"

Splat! The noodle rope broke, and Cole fell on top of a guard.

"Got you!" shouted the guard. Cole burped in his face.

The guard dragged Cole through the factory and threw him into a jail cell.

Cole grinned. "It was all worth it"—he lifted the guard's keys into the air—"for these!"

"Cole?" murmured Zane. Cole was leaning over his friend, unlocking his chains. "You have returned."

Cole smiled. "Of course. I made a promise. Now, c'mere, you shiny, new tin can." He hugged his friend. "Can you feel the love?"

"No," Zane said honestly. "But the longer we stand here, the less time we have to escape."

"You were always the smart one," Cole said. "Let's go!"

Meanwhile, Nya had sneaked into Chen's study and was examining the Book of Spells. "Page 102 . . . 122 . . . 149. This changes everything!"

Nya tore the page out of the book. Then she heard footsteps.

Outside in the hallway, a guard said, "There's been a breach in the factory. Master Cole has gone missing."

Clouse cackled. "Release my pet. She'll make sure he doesn't escape."

Down in the tunnels, Zane and Cole were lost. "Not that way. That will only take us back to where we started," said Zane.

Suddenly, there was a rattling sound.

"We need to move!" shouted Cole. "Trust me, you'll want to keep up."

Zane swung his head around and met Clouse's pet—an enormous serpent!

Zane and Cole ran as fast as they could. But they kept bumping into the serpent's scaly body.

"Another dead end," said Cole.

"The serpent's strategy appears to be to surround us and coil inward," noted Zane. "Very clever."

"Yeah, well, my strategy is not to be eaten!" cried Cole.

"Pixal: Calculate escape scenarios," Zane said. Pixal was a Nindroid whose hard drive was hidden inside Zane's head.

"Calculating escape routes. Activating explosives," she replied.

"Pixal?" Cole said. "You've got a *girl* stuck in your head?"

Zane tossed a handful of explosives in a circle, creating a hole for him and Cole to fall through. *Boom!*

"I'm gonna like the new you," Cole said.

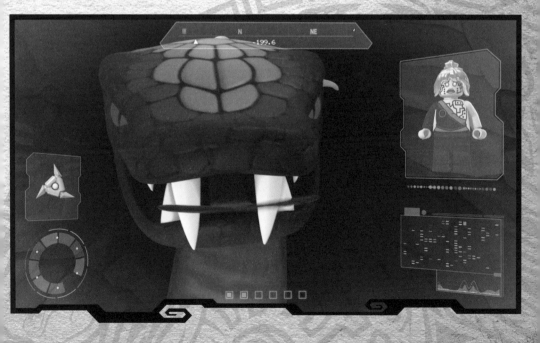

SPY GAMES

Upstairs, Jay, Kai, and Lloyd were meeting with the Elemental Masters. "No one leaves this room until we find out who's passing information to Chen," said Lloyd.

Neuro began reading minds. "Someone here isn't who they say they are."

Skylor cut in. "Maybe I should use your power and see inside your head."

"This is what Chen wants!" Kai said. "For us to fight. There has to be a better way."

Garmadon nodded. "There is. Everyone who's ever worked for Chen has an Anacondrai tattoo on their back. Find the tattoo, find the spy."

Neuro stepped forward to show everyone his back was bare.

"Who's next?" asked Lloyd.

Back in the banquet hall, Chen was enjoying a Kabuki performance. Nya slipped into the room. She hid the spell page inside her kimono. Then she tried to fit in with the other dancers.

"Tell me they've caught the escaped prisoner," Chen growled at Clouse.

"Not yet," Clouse said. "But I have far worse news: Someone has stolen the spell!"

"Do you need the page to do the spell?" Chen asked.

Clouse shook his head. "No. But if the ninja find it, the fighters will know we've lied."

"Then we must find that page!" Chen cried.

Clouse looked at the spell book. There was a white smudge on the cover—Kabuki makeup! "We have a spy! Guards, search every servant in this room!"

THE SPY HUNT

Loud music interrupted the search for the spy. Dareth had accidentally flipped a switch, and now his favorite rock music was blasting all over the island.

"That sound is coming from the spy," said Chen. "Find the signal, find the spy!"

"You heard him: Search the island!" Clouse ordered. He turned to Nya and the other Kabuki. "As for you . . . stay put."

The ninja were still seeking the spy in their midst.

"Only two left," said Lloyd, looking at Skylor and Shade.

"I hate to do this," Kai said to Skylor. "But can I see your back, please?"

"Wait!" Lloyd interrupted. "Where did Shade go?"

"He's disappearing through his own shadow!" said Jay.

"I ain't your spy, and I ain't your friend, either. That staff will be mine!" Shade hissed.

Everyone scrambled to catch Shade. But he dodged them all and disappeared.

Kai turned to Skylor. "Sorry I didn't trust you."

"If you still think I'm the spy, watch me walk out that door," Skylor replied. As she strode out, Kai could see there was no tattoo on her back.

In the banquet hall, Chen sighed happily. "Kabuki are always pleased to serve me."

Nya fanned Chen and pretended she was happy to serve. She had to, or Chen would know *she* was the spy.

"Have you found where the signal's coming from?" Chen asked Clouse.

"We haven't found anything on the island yet," said Clouse. "But we will."

Nya slipped away from Chen and called Dareth. "Dareth! They're coming! Do you read me? They're coming for you!"

Dareth looked out the mobile unit's window. "*Ahh!* Where's the cloak button?" He pressed a few buttons, but it was too late. The guards were almost on him.

Dareth revved the motor. "Now, let's test what's under this hood!"

The guards dove out of the way as Dareth blasted toward them. Blade chariots and copters began chasing him.

Trouble was, Dareth had no idea how to drive his getaway car. "Somebody get me outta here!" he screamed.

On command, a mini-robot popped up and took over the steering wheel. "Autopilot: initiated."

"Score one for the Brown Ninja!" Dareth whooped as he took down a blade chariot. Then he realized the mini-robot was driving them toward a cliff. "Bad autopilot! Bad!"

Dareth slammed on the brakes, and the mobile unit skidded onto its side. There was no escape—he was surrounded.

"Nya, I've been taken hostage! You're on your own."

Back in Chen's lair, Nya's comm unit lit up.
Chen could hear everything Dareth was saying!
"So *you're* the spy," Chen said, grabbing her.
"The spell!"
Nya wiggled away from him. "By the way,
your feet stink!"
Chen grabbed his staff and shot ice at her.
But Nya was too fast.
"Get her. And get that spell!" Chen shouted.

Down in the tunnels, Zane and Cole hid as two guards passed. "We have to find the spy. Forget about the escaped factory worker; Chen will make the other workers pay," one guard told the other.

"I have to go back," Cole whispered. "A ninja protects those who cannot protect themselves."

Zane nodded. "And a ninja never leaves another ninja's side."

Cole smiled. "We'll get off this island, Zane. But it's either all of us or none of us."

Outside the palace, Nya kept running as Clouse and the guards chased her.

Clouse grabbed for her, but Nya kicked him away. Then she raced up a rooftop and found cover in the forest below. She was gone!

"Find her!" Clouse screamed to the guards.

A guard hurried into Chen's throne room.

"My spy, have they found the girl?" Chen asked.

"No," said the guard. "But you have a bigger problem." The guard began to change shape. It was Skylor! "Cole's got the Ninja of Ice, Father."

Chen smiled. "Thank you, daughter. The Master of Form's power has proved useful to you. The ninja's time here is done. Tomorrow, we will break up the ninja . . . forever!"

A DANGEROUS QUEST

Cole, Jay, Kai, and Zane were on a dangerous quest. They were racing to find the powerful Realm Crystal before Morro, the ghostly Master of Wind, could find it.

The ninja were also searching for Lloyd, whose form Morro had taken over. His friends hoped that if they found the crystal, they would also be able to rescue Lloyd.

The ninja were deep under the ocean in *Airship Rex*. The secret entrance to the Tomb of the First Spinjitzu Master was far below the water's surface. The Realm Crystal was hidden somewhere in the tomb.

Sensei Wu spoke to the ninja on their monitor. "Find the Realm Crystal before Morro does."

The ninja knew this would be difficult. They had lost their elemental powers when Morro escaped the Cursed Realm. Plus, they had to complete a series of challenges to reach the crystal.

Jay gulped. "Cole's a ghost, Kai can't swim, we have no magical sword, no elemental powers . . . What could go wrong?"

Onscreen, Misako shared some words of advice. "I have discovered a riddle that may help you in the tomb: A Spinjitzu Master can. A Spinjitzu Master cannot. To move forward, don't look ahead to find his resting spot."

"That's food for thought," Cole said.

"Speaking of food," Jay yelped. "We're about to be some!"

There was a giant octopus on their tail!

"We have to go faster!" Kai said.

"Hold on!" Cole blasted the ship into high gear.

"What kind of weapons does this thing have?" Jay asked.

"We don't need weapons," Zane said, pointing. "Aim for that rock!"

Cole steered their ship through a hole in the giant rock. The octopus followed—but it was too big. It got stuck.

"Thatta boy, *Rex*! Thatta boy!" cheered Jay.

A few minutes later, *Rex* floated up into the mouth of the underground tomb, and the ninja scrambled out. Jay spotted a piece of Morro's robes torn on a rock. The Master of Wind was already there!

"There goes any hope Morro couldn't find this place." Jay sighed.

"Hey, stay positive," Kai reminded him. "We're about to risk our lives going through traps, and all we have to rely on is one another. We're lucky we got this far."

THE TOMB OF THE FIRST SPINJITZU MASTER

"The First Spinjitzu Master," Cole said, gazing up at a giant statue. "Creator of all Ninjago."

Suddenly, a computer voice behind them said, "Destination reached. Auto return initiated." *Rex* powered up and disappeared.

"Auto return?" Jay shrieked. "No! Bad *Rex*!"

"Our weapons were in there," Zane said.

Kai sighed. "No sword, no powers, no problem. We can do this, guys. As long as we got one another."

The ninja made their way down a long hallway. At the end, a stone door opened. Inside a round room, there were sixteen more doors.

"This could be the first test," Cole said.

"We're supposed to pick a door," Kai said. "But which one?"

"What was it Misako said?" Jay asked.

Zane repeated the riddle: "'A Spinjitzu Master can. A Spinjitzu Master cannot. To move forward, don't look ahead to find his resting spot.'"

"A Spinjitzu Master can what?" Kai asked.

"Sixteen doors for sixteen realms?" Jay suggested.

Cole nodded. "Could be. Let me guess: Pick the wrong door and we'll be in a realm of hurt."

"We can figure this out," Kai said, focusing. "'A Spinjitzu Master can . . . can . . .'"

Jay pointed to one of the doors. "The symbol above this door—it's a tornado! 'A Spinjitzu Master can.' This could be the one, right?" He reached for the handle.

"Jay, wait!" Zane shouted. He was getting a message from Pixal. "Step away from that door."

"What is it?" Jay asked.

"We're inside a zoetrope," Zane told him. "The engravings create a moving image when the room spins."

"I don't get it," said Cole.

"'A Spinjitzu Master can . . .'" Kai blurted. "We need to do Spinjitzu!"

Zane began to turn around and around. *Ninja-go!* As he spun, the sixteen different images blended together to look like one.

"That's the one," Zane said, pointing to a door with a curved symbol. "That's the door out."

"I dunno, Zane," said Cole. "Isn't that the same door we came in? Are you sure?"

"Do you really want to doubt a Nindroid?" asked Zane.

Kai stepped forward. "Open the door. Let's find out."

Jay pushed the door open, revealing a large cavern. At the far end of the room, a golden staff glowed on a pedestal.

"That wasn't here before," Cole said. "How can this be the way if it's the same way we came in?"

Kai marched forward. "Welcome to the Tomb of the First Spinjitzu Master."

Jay smiled at Zane. "Nice one, Zane. Who needs the Sword of Sanctuary when you've got a Nindroid?"

SPY GAMES

"The staff of the First Spinjitzu Master," Kai said.

"This is the second test," Cole said. "Zane, what do you think?"

Zane scanned his inner computer. "Pixal can see no pattern. For this room, I'm at a loss."

"The first test was 'a Spinjitzu Master CAN,'" said Jay. "So this one's 'a Spinjitzu Master CANNOT.' I'm not sure I like the sound of that . . ."

Zane stepped forward. His foot triggered a booby trap. The ninja leaped out of the way as darts flew at them!

"That was a close one," Zane said.

"Every step is a trap," Jay groaned.

"I suspect the golden staff is a lever to deactivate the traps," Zane said. "How does one reach the staff if it becomes more difficult to get there with every step?"

"So if a Spinjitzu Master cannot do it, how are we supposed to reach the staff?" Cole wondered.

Kai raced toward the staff, flipping and spinning through the air. "Watch and learn!"

Kai darted across the room. But every time he got near the staff, he set off more traps. Spikes shot at him. Flames blazed. Rocks swung from the ceiling. "I can make it," Kai grunted.

He kept his eyes on the prize even as pieces of the floor crumbled away. With every step he took, the room became more dangerous. "Okay," Kai finally admitted. "Maybe I can't."

"Will you please stop moving?!" Jay screamed.

"I can make it!" Kai shouted, sure of himself again. "It's just a hop, skip, and a jump." He crouched low to leap toward the staff—but then he slipped. The ground beneath him fell away, and he had to scramble to safety.

"I dunno how much more we can take," Cole said, shaking his head.

"The riddle clearly said this is a test a Spinjitzu Master cannot do," Jay said. "So why aren't we listening to the riddle?"

"Wait!" Cole had an idea. "What if it's a trick? What if the reason we can't do it is because we were never meant to reach the staff? What's the first rule of being a ninja?"

"A ninja never quits," Zane said.

"Exactly," Cole nodded. "That's why we can't do it. Because a ninja would never give up."

"What are you saying?" Kai asked. "We just quit? Are you insane?"

"Trust me," Cole said. Then he jumped into the dark pit below.

"Cole!" Jay, Kai, and Zane screamed.

Cole's voice faded away in the darkness. Then he hollered from down below. "Woo-hoo! Come on down and enjoy the ride!"

"He's okay," Zane cheered. He, Kai, and Jay all jumped into the blackness. A moment later, the ninja were slipping down a long, ice slide.

"Try to stay together," Kai said.

"Stay *together*?" Jay shrieked. "I'm just trying to stay in one piece!"

THE MAZE

At the bottom, the ninja spilled out into a giant, icy cavern.

"Is everyone okay?" Zane asked.

Kai shook his head. "What did we get ourselves into?"

"It's a maze!" Jay said happily. "I'm great at mazes! The trick with mazes is, if you follow the wall, you'll eventually find your way out. Just don't make any drastic turns."

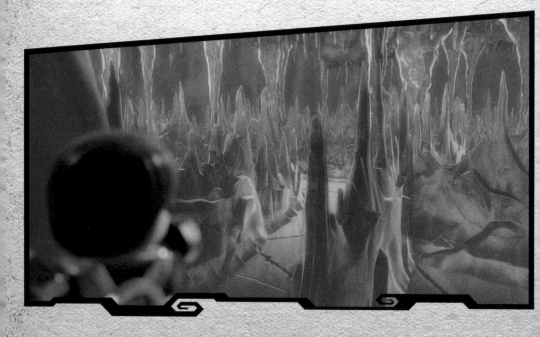

"Whoa," Kai said. He peered into one of the icy walls and saw his own reflection—but he was much older! "The maze is showing us what we'll look like in the future!"

Cole gasped. "Why can't I see my reflection?"

"Probably because you're a ghost," Kai said.

Zane shook his head. "Ghosts cast reflections, Kai. He's just looking in the wrong place."

"I'm looking at the same place you are!" Cole yelped. "So why can you all see yourselves, but I'm completely gone? Am I not gonna make it?!"

"Hey, guys," Jay said. "Guess what? In the future, I get an awesome eye patch!"

Cole rubbed at the wall again, trying to see himself. But instead, he saw someone else. A reflection—and then the icy wall shattered.

"It's Morro!" Cole screamed. "He's still in Lloyd's body, and he's in the maze, too!"

"All you ninja do is talk," Morro hissed. "Blah, blah, blah. I'll stop you from talking!"

Morro chased Jay through the maze. He slashed at him with his sword. "He's attacking an unarmed man!" Jay called out.

"We're coming for you!" Kai promised.

Cole, Kai, and Zane raced after Morro and Jay. When they caught up, the Master of Wind growled at them. He was strong enough to fight all four ninja at once. Especially when the ninja had no powers or weapons!

Suddenly, Kai had an idea. He'd noticed that every time Morro's sword cut through an ice wall, two more walls grew back in its place.

"Catch me if you can!" Kai said, dashing away.

Morro raced after Kai, slashing his blade at any walls in his way. Dozens of new ones sprouted up around him. Before long, he was trapped in an icy prison of his own making.

"You can't trap me, ninja," Morro yelled. "I'll find you. Just wait, you'll see!"

THE FINAL RIDDLE

"How do we get out of here?" Jay asked.

Cole thought about the riddle again. "'To move forward, don't look ahead . . .'"

"Don't look ahead." Jay said. "Look below!"

"There's light," Kai said, looking through the icy floor below them. "Everyone, dig!"

Cole, Jay, Kai, and Zane dug through the floor and fell into another hidden chamber.

At the bottom, they all stopped. The bones of an ancient ninja lay before them, along with a simple headstone.

"It's him," Kai said, bowing. "The First Spinjitzu Master."

"The Realm Crystal," Zane said. He gently pried the crystal out of the skeleton's hands.

"How does it work?" Kai asked.

Morro's evil laugh rang out overhead. "How it works is . . . you'll hand over the crystal, or say good-bye to your friend!"

Morro had finally left Lloyd's body—and now he had a sword to Lloyd's throat!

"I'm sorry," Lloyd moaned. "I couldn't stop him."

"So what'll it be?" Morro asked. "The crystal or your friend?"

"If we hand him the crystal, he'll curse Ninjago and every other realm," Zane whispered.

"But look at Lloyd—he's too weak to protect himself," Cole said.

"Both options totally stink," Jay muttered.

"Give me the Realm Crystal or else!" Morro shouted.

"Our powers," Kai said suddenly. "Now that Morro's out of Lloyd's body, our powers are starting to come back!"

"Yeah, but they're weak," Jay noted. "And we're in no position to fight back now."

Kai clenched his fists, holding the Realm Crystal tight. "Leave that to me . . . Be ready." He yelled up to Morro, "We'll give you the Realm Crystal!"

Kai squeezed the crystal in his hand and
threw it. When Morro caught it, it burned him.
Kai had used his fire power to heat it up!

With a roar of pain, Morro dropped the
crystal . . . straight into the roaring river below.
"The crystal," he howled. Furious, Morro pushed
Lloyd into the water.

"Lloyd!" the ninja screamed. The river was
dragging Lloyd into raging rapids.

Kai and Cole ran after Lloyd. "But I can't get
to him," Kai wailed. "I can't swim!"

"You can't swim?" Cole asked. "I can't touch
the water! I'm a ghost, remember?"

While Cole and Kai chased Lloyd, Jay
and Zane took on Morro. Zane shot a blast
of water at Morro's sword, freezing it solid.

"Nice one, Zane!" Jay called out.

Downriver, Lloyd was getting closer and
closer to the rapids. Kai leaped after him!

"Kai's got Lloyd!" Jay yelled. "But who's
got Kai?"

Cole reached over the edge. With a
mighty tug, he pulled both Kai and Lloyd
out just before they plunged into the pit of
bubbling lava below.

A moment later, the Realm Crystal sailed over the waterfall.

Suddenly, it slowed and hovered in midair. Then it soared upward again! Using the power of the wind, Morro pulled the Realm Crystal straight into his own hands. He fled with the stone.

"Get him, everyone!" Cole cried.

But it was too late. Morro was gone—and so was the crystal.

The ninja raced out of the tomb just in time to see Morro disappear. They had failed in their quest to get the crystal.

"You all sacrificed so much to save me," Lloyd said gratefully. "But now Ninjago's going to be cursed."

"But we have you," Zane said, putting his hand on his shoulder.

"And our powers are back," Jay said.

"As you get strong, so will we," Cole vowed. He looked at his brothers and smiled. "They haven't seen us at full strength yet!"

SIX NEW CELEBRITIES

"Cut!" cried Dareth. He and the ninja were on the set of their new TV commercial. "That acting *knocked me out*. You ninja are the hottest thing in Ninjago City!"

Dareth was right. After destroying the Cursed Realm, the ninja had become more famous than ever.

In fact, Cole, Jay, Kai, Lloyd, Nya, and Zane couldn't go anywhere without drawing crowds. Whenever they were out in New Ninjago City, they had to hide from their fans.

Most of the ninja preferred the privacy of the *Destiny's Bounty.* But Kai loved having fans follow him around.

Onboard the *Bounty*, Cole was focused on his training.

"When one is a ghost," Wu said. "One may have new abilities. Focus and discover them."

Cole closed his eyes. He floated up into the air — and then disappeared. A moment later, he appeared again. "Did you see me?" he yelled. "I disappeared! I mean, did you *not* see me?"

"Very good, Cole," Wu said. "That's it for today."

A NEW MISSION

A few minutes later, Misako and Wu called the ninja together.

"What is it?" Kai asked. "Have the stores sold out of Kai action figures?"

"No," said Wu. "When you destroyed the Cursed Realm, one ghost escaped. And you know him all too well . . . Clouse."

"Clouse, the evil sorcerer from Chen's island?" Cole gasped.

"Yes. Security footage shows him buying a train ticket to Stiix," said Wu. "Go there and stop whatever it is he is planning to do."

"But Dareth wanted us to visit the hospital for that Grant-a-Wish thing," said Kai.

Lloyd cut him off. "We take orders from Master Wu, not Dareth. Lil' Nelson only has a broken leg. If his wish is to be a 'Ninja for a Day,' that day can be tomorrow. Let's suit up!"

A few minutes later, the ninja were soaring toward Stiix on their dragons.

"We're flying over Ninjago City," Kai said. "What do you say we drop by to see Lil' Nelson?"

"We don't have time," Lloyd said.

"Technically, we do as long as we do not encounter any problems," Zane said.

NINJA FOR A DAY

At the hospital, the ninja went straight to Lil' Nelson's room. "As a part of the Grant-a-Wish Foundation, we dub you an honorary ninja for the day," Lloyd told him.

"Could you stay and sign the other kids' casts?" Lil Nelson asked.

"Wish we could," Nya said, "but duty calls."

Cole pointed out the window. Screaming fans and TV crews had surrounded the hospital. "Uh-oh. Looks like we've got company!"

"I don't see us flying out of here with these birds in the sky," Cole said. He pointed to a crew of news helicopters.

Lloyd nodded. "Cole's right. No dragons. If we're going to escape, we can't be followed."

"So what do we do?" Cole asked.

Lil' Nelson whipped around in his wheelchair. "You say I'm a ninja for the day . . . let me get you out of here! Call me *the Purple Ninja!*"

"This is as far as I can take you," Lil' Nelson said. "Follow the stairs to the rooftop. From there, take back streets. I'll hold them off here."

"Lil' Nelson," said Lloyd. "I mean, Purple Ninja . . . thanks."

"Thank *you*," Lil' Nelson said. "You made my wish come true."

"Looks like we lost them," Cole said as the ninja scrambled up to the roof.

"But the nearest rooftop is still too far to jump," said Kai. "Airjitzu?"

Nya shook her head. "I just learned how to make a water dragon. I haven't earned my Airjitzu suit yet."

"If we don't leave now, we'll never get to Stiix in time to stop Clouse," said Zane.

"We're a team," Jay said. "We stick together. Take my hand, Nya."

Nya shook her head. "Thanks, but I can stick up for myself."

"They're going to see us," said Lloyd. "Quick — take cover!"

"Just take his hand, Nya," yelled Cole. "Or else we're gonna be spotted!"

He and the other ninja leaped up and hid behind a huge sign. But it was too late. The helicopters were back . . . and Nya was right out in the open.

"Let's hope Clouse missed his train," said Lloyd.

"Now what?" asked Cole.

One of the choppers spun around. Dareth was inside!

"This could be a big scoop." Dareth said. "Hop in!"

CLOUSE ON THE LOOSE

Meanwhile, in the village of Stiix, Clouse was hunting through heaps of trash. He had traveled a long way to find something very special.

"No . . ." muttered the ghostly sorcerer as he dug through the junk. "No . . . no . . ."

Suddenly, Clouse pulled a filthy teapot out of the rubble. "Yes! The Teapot of Tyrahn!"

Clouse rubbed the side of the teapot. "Work, darn you!" he screamed. He twisted the pot, trying to line up a series of markings.

Suddenly, the teapot began to glow. Clouse dropped it and backed away.

RETURN OF THE DJINN

Smoke flowed out of the pot. Then a shadowy figure appeared. It was Nadakhan the Djinn, one of the most famous pirates of all time. He had been trapped inside the teapot for years.

"I'm free?" Nadakhan asked. "Where am I? What year is it?"

"Nadakhan?" Clouse clapped. "I've freed a genie!"

"I prefer the term 'djinn,'" Nadakhan growled.

"Who cares?" Clouse said. "I want my three wishes!"

Nadakhan nodded. "I must warn you. You cannot wish for love, death, and most certainly —"

Clouse cut him off. "More wishes. Yeah, yeah, I know the rules." He stepped forward. "I wish for my Book of Spells!"

"Your wish is yours to keep," said Nadakhan. A moment later, Clouse's spell book appeared.

"Ha!" Clouse said happily. "With my spells, who needs more wishes?" But when he touched the book, it burst into flames. "What's happening?"

Nadakhan chuckled. "You should have known the book was thrown into a fire. Perhaps you should wish for more than a pile of ash." He smirked. "Now for your second wish?"

Clouse considered. "I can't defeat the ninja as a ghost. I wish to be mortal again!"

"Your wish is yours to keep," Nadakhan murmured.

Clouse stared at his hands. They were becoming solid right before his eyes. "Yes! It's working. I can *feel* again."

But suddenly, he was overcome with pain. "Agh! My hands, my head . . . the pain!"

Nadakhan laughed. "Yes, you can feel. Becoming physical is a painful process. I wish it would be over soon, but it won't. You could . . . wish it all away.

"Wish it all to go away and you will be free from your pain, free from your poor choices, free from existence," Nadakhan went on.

"I wish it all to go away!" Clouse screamed.

Nadakhan chuckled. "Your wish is yours to keep."

Gold dust poured out of Nadakhan's teapot. It surrounded Clouse and began to suck him inside the teapot!

"Be careful what you wish for!" Nadakhan said.

PRACTICALLY PRICELESS?

A few minutes later, the ninja had finally arrived in Stiix. They put on disguises to avoid being recognized. Then they began searching for Clouse.

After half an hour, the ninja regrouped. "He isn't here," Zane said.

"He could be long gone by now," said Cole.

Kai grinned. "But look what I found in the trash! A Kai action figure. No way anyone threw this out. It's practically priceless."

Lloyd pulled out his communicator. "No sign of Clouse," he told Misako.

"Keep looking," Misako told him. "Wu's at the Library of Domu trying to figure out what Clouse is looking for. If I hear anything, you'll be the first to know."

"Look!" Jay said, giggling as he poked around a junk heap. "Another Kai doll. There's dozens!"

Back in New Ninjago City, Nadakhan was having a hard time understanding a world that had changed since he'd been trapped in his teapot.

"You look lost. Can I be of assistance?" said a voice.

Nadakhan spun around. A computer with a display of Cyrus Borg's head was behind him.

"You are talking to Info-Vision," the voice explained. "Ask a question, and maybe I can answer it."

"Where is my crew, from *Misfortune's Keep*?" Nadakhan growled.

An image of a pirate ship appeared on screen. "The captain of *Misfortune's Keep*, Nadakhan the Djinn, was trapped in the Teapot of Tyrahn. His crew was marooned in separate realms."

"How do I get to these realms?" asked Nadakhan.

"You need the Realm Crystal. It is under the protection of the Masters of Spinjitzu," the computer replied.

"Tell me how to find them!" Nadakhan ordered.

WANTED: SIX NINJA

Back in Stiix, the ninja still hadn't found Clouse. So they stopped for lunch at a canteen.

A news report blared on TV. "They're calling it the crime wave of the century. Lloyd Garmadon was just caught on tape robbing the city bank. And at Mega Monster Amusement Park, Zane was on a rampage."

"Someone's pretending to be us!" Jay gasped.

"But who?" wondered Cole.

"The ninja are at large," a policeman said on the screen. "They are armed and dangerous. If you see them, call local law enforcement."

"Maybe now's a good time to leave?" Kai said.

"Hey," said one of the other customers, eyeing Zane. "Aren't you . . ."

"No!" Jay said quickly. "We're that other group with a Nindroid, a ghost, a girl, and uh . . ."

Jay and the other ninja backed away as a mob of customers came after them.

"Six on six," Kai said. "At least it's even numbers."

Lloyd shook his head. "We're not going to fight. Right now it's us who look like the bad guys."

"How are we supposed to defend ourselves?" Jay asked. "Witty banter?"

"Run!" cried Nya. She and the other ninja raced along the boardwalk, then up and over rooftops.

At the edge of a rooftop, the ninja had to use Airjitzu to get back on the ground. Jay held out his hand, offering Nya help. This time, she took it. "Thanks," she said.

The ninja ran again. But the crowd of villagers was close on their heels. "There's nowhere to hide!" Cole cried.

"There may be one place . . ." Kai said.

Kai used Spinjitzu to bore a hole through the floorboards. He and the others dropped under the boardwalk. Then they leaped across beams under the village.

"Mom," Lloyd said into his communicator. "We're in a bit of a jam!"

"I saw the news," Misako called back. "I am en route. Looks like you've gone from fame to framed."

The ninja watched as the *Destiny's Bounty* raced over a bluff. Suddenly, a police officer yelled, "Take her down!" He fired a grappling gun and snared the *Bounty*!

The ninja's ship was trapped — and the ninja were surrounded.

"We have a better chance of getting out of here if we split up," Lloyd said.

"But nothing good ever comes when we're split up," said Jay.

"We have no choice," Lloyd replied. He and the ninja fled in six different directions.

Back in the Library of Domu, Wu didn't know the ninja were in danger. But he *had* figured out what Clouse was searching for in Stiix.

Wu scanned the book in his hands, reading about the Teapot of Tyrahn. *"Be careful what you wish for.* Hmm."

Behind him, Nadakhan chuckled. "Did somebody say *wish*?"

THE HOLIDAY SPIRIT

"The Day of the Departed is my favorite holiday," sighed Nya, the Water Ninja. "I love all the lights!"

"And the costumes," said Kai, the Fire Ninja.

"And candy!" Jay, the Lightning Ninja, said through a mouthful of treats.

Master Wu nodded. "Yes, enjoy the fun and festivities. But never lose sight of the true meaning of the Day of the Departed." He smiled at Misako and the six ninja. "We light these lanterns to remember our ancestors. And to settle our debts."

"Ninja! Master Wu! Come!" cried Dr. Sander Saunders, the head of the Ninjago Museum of History. "Might I present our newest exhibit . . . the Hall of Villainy!"

The group walked into a room filled with statues of the most terrible villains the ninja had ever fought. "We have Samukai! Chen! Kozu! Cryptor! Morro! This exhibit is opening on the Day of Departed — and there is also a lunar eclipse."

Wu nodded. "The rarest Yin-Yang Eclipse."

"Scary holiday, scary exhibit, scary moon," Dr. Saunders said. "Magic is in the air!"

Cole, the Earth Ninja, read the card in front of Master Yang's portrait. "Yang will be remembered as the creator of Airjitzu." Cole shook his head. "*I* remember him as the guy who turned me into a ghost!" He looked down at a glowing blade inside a case. "Hey, Dr. Saunders, what's the story on this thing?"

But no one heard him. "Hello?" Cole called. Since he'd turned into a ghost, Cole often felt invisible. "It's like I don't exist anymore." He glared up at Master Yang's portrait. "And it's all your fault!"

THE DEPARTED

"The Yin Blade belonged to Master Yang," Dr. Saunders told the other ninja. "It is said to possess much Dark Magic. That's why it's sealed in this case made of ClearStone. No living being can get through it."

"*Cole . . .*" a voice called quietly. Master Yang's portrait began to glow. "Cole . . . *come*. Close the circle."

"Tell me you heard that," Cole said to his friends. But the other ninja were gone.

"They don't even realize I'm gone," Cole grumbled. "Maybe *I'm* departed."

"If we never look to the past, we cannot see the future. On the Day of the Departed, we pause to remember those we've lost," Master Wu told the ninja.

Everyone scattered. Each had people to remember.

Zane used his ice powers to build an ice sculpture of his creator, Dr. Julien, in the forest.

Kai and Nya lit a lantern in honor of their parents.

Lloyd and Misako visited the statue of Garmadon.

Jay set off to spend the afternoon with his parents.
But Cole had a different plan for this Day of the
Departed. He went to visit Master Yang in his haunted
temple. Wu had said the Day of the Departed was a
day for settling debts — and Cole and Yang had a
serious debt to settle!

"All right, Yang," Cole called. He held up the Yin
Blade he'd taken from the Ninjago Museum of History.
"Show yourself!"

NIGHT OF THE RETURN?

"The Yin Blade!" Master Yang gasped. "What are you going to do?"

"There's magic in the air," Cole told him. "So I'm settling my debt!" He swung the Yin Blade at Yang.

Master Yang leaped to the side. The blade sliced through a stone orb as the moon entered its eclipse. Moonlight hit the orb, and bright green fog flowed out.

"You never should have played with Dark Magic, boy. This Day of the Departed will be remembered as my Night of the Return!" Yang cackled.

The green fog poured out of Yang's ghostly temple. The wind carried the fog into Ninjago City, where it flooded the Hall of Villainy. Suddenly, all the statues came to life!

"What has brought us back?" Master Chen asked.

"Perhaps *he* can explain," Morro said.

Yang spoke from his portrait on the wall. "My magic has brought you back from the Departed Realm. But you can only remain for the eclipse . . . unless you destroy the ninja who destroyed you. Do that, and you will take their places among the living.

"The ninja are spread around Ninjago," Yang told them. "You must each choose one and—"

"I call Zane!" yelled Samukai.

"The blacksmith's brats are mine!" called Chen.

"How come you get two?" asked Pythor, who just happened to be visiting the Hall of Villainy.

"Time is wasting," Yang snapped. "And I've got my own thing going on. So work it out!"

"Master Wu and I left things unfinished," said Morro. "I will settle our debt once and for all."

Back at Yang's temple, Cole was in trouble. "So . . . guys," he said to Yang's ghostly students, who were guarding him. "What say you help me out?"

"Your pleas are useless," Yang told him. "My students are loyal to no one but me."

"C'mon, guys!" Cole said, begging. "Yang is, like, the definition of evil."

Master Yang shook his head. "Actually, *Yang* means *good*. But I always did aspire for *great* . . . "

YANG'S CURSE

"I dedicated my life to the study of martial arts," Yang told him. "I mastered them all, and even created my own. Airjitzu was my first achievement, but it was nothing compared to finding the Yin Blade. The blade's magic is so powerful, it's said to hold the key to eternal life. But when I tested its powers on myself, something went . . . wrong."

Yang hung his head. "So while I will live forever, it is only as a ghost. Cursed to haunt this temple. Never able to return. Until tonight, thanks to you."

Yang smiled at Cole. "On the Day of the Departed, when there's a Yin-Yang Eclipse, the Yin Blade can cut the Rift of Return."

"You won't get away with this," Cole spat. "When my friends see I'm missing, they'll come for me!"

"See you're missing?" Yang snorted. "You can barely see yourself. Besides, you've caused a few problems for your friends . . . " He laughed gleefully. "There's no one to help you. Now excuse me . . . I have a rift to open."

Alone in his monastery, Wu sensed something was wrong. "An eclipse is always an omen," he said, looking up at the moon. "But is this one a sign of good or bad?"

Suddenly, Morro appeared behind him.

"Bad. *Very* bad," the Master of Wind whispered ominously.

All the ninja were in trouble.

When Nya and Kai stepped outside their parents' old blacksmith shop, they discovered one of their worst enemies had returned.

"Chen?!" Nya cried. "I don't know how you're here, but it's two against one."

"Is it?" Chen asked, giggling, as more villains appeared behind him.

Kai and Nya exchanged a look. This was not going to be an easy fight . . .

Meanwhile, Zane faced off against Cryptor and the Nindroids in the forest.

"Escape is futile, Zane," Cryptor growled. "You and I share programming. I know your every move before you even make it."

Zane smiled. He called on his friend Pixal, the android who shared his neural drive. Together, the pair tried to trick Cryptor, but they couldn't.

"Enjoy the Departed Realm," Cryptor said. "Oh, and say hi to dear old Dad!"

   While Zane was trying to beat Cryptor, Jay was
trying to protect his parents from the wrath of Samukai.
   "I got this, Dad," Jay said, stepping forward. "Samukai,
I have no idea what you want with my parents —"
   Samukai cut him off. "It's not your parents I want, Jay.
It's *you*!"
   "Bring it!" Jay yelled. He pulled out his nunchuks and
leaped into battle.

Back at Yang's temple, Cole raced through the hallways, searching for Yang. As he ran, he battled Yang's students one by one — until the only person left to stop was Yang himself.

Cole spotted the ghostly Master of Airjitzu at the top of a ladder. "I'm coming for you, Yang!" he called. "It's over. You don't have any more students to help you. You're all alone."

"I am not alone," Yang laughed as more students surrounded them. "Not at all."

Cole sighed. "Kinda wishing I wasn't alone, either . . ."

AN UNEXPECTED ALLY

Far from the temple, Wu faced off against Morro. "We have fought twice before. Though it pains me, I will do so again if I must."

Morro shook his head. "I'm not here to fight you," he told Wu. "I'm here to warn you. Master Yang has put your team in terrible danger. He has made you forget one of your own."

"Tell me more," Wu said.

"I will," Morro agreed. "But let's do it aboard the *Destiny's Bounty*. We have to warn the others."

Onboard the *Bounty*, Wu and Morro set off to alert the ninja. But the ninja were already busy battling their greatest enemies . . . and winning.

Outside their parents' old home, Nya and Kai climbed aboard Nya's speeder. Chen, Eyezore, and Zugu were hot on their trail.

"Duck!" Nya yelled to her brother as she raced under a tree. Though Chen and his partners were fierce, the brother and sister duo fought off all three villains!

"Can't . . . hold . . . on!" Lloyd grunted under the weight of a huge statue Pythor had used to trap him.

"You always underestimate me," Pythor taunted. "You're so like your father."

Misako nodded. "He's right, Lloyd. You're brave. And noble. And —"

Lloyd glanced up at the statue of his father, Garmadon, on the hillside above him. He took a deep breath. "And a master of Spinjitzu! You're still with me, Dad." Lloyd cast the statue off and spun toward Pythor. "*Ninjaaaaa-GO!*"

Deep in the forest, Zane had survived his fight with Cryptor and the Nindroids. But now Cryptor had Zane trapped, and there was nothing Pixal could do to help.

"It's no use fighting," Cryptor said. "I know your every move, Zane. And I know you never give up."

Zane had to fight differently if he wanted to win. He released his weapons. "Then I give up."

Cryptor swung his TechnoBlade at Zane, who leaped over it. The blade swung back at Cryptor, and he vanished in a puff of smoke. Zane and Pixal had won!

"This isn't personal, Jay," Samukai said, standing over Jay. "It's only so I can return to the living world. As soon as this is over, I'll release your parents."

"I'm on that!" yelled a voice from inside a huge mech. A metal arm pulled Jay's parents to safety.

"Ronin!" Jay whooped, spotting his friend inside the mech. "Thanks for coming to help."

"Uh, yeah . . . " Ronin said slowly. "I came to help. I definitely wasn't here to, um, 'borrow' some scrap metal for my mech while everyone was celebrating."

THE RIFT OPENS

Master Yang stood outside his temple, waiting to return to the living world.

"Yes! It is working!" Yang raised his Yin Blade toward the moon. "Close the circle . . . open the rift!"

The time was near. It wouldn't be long now . . .

Yang reached up his arms as the Rift of Return opened. "Freedom — it's all mine!"

But before Yang could fly through, Cole grabbed him. "No!" he cried.

Back in Ninjago City, the other ninja met up on the steps of the Ninjago Museum of History.

"Guys!" Jay panted. "I have the ghost story to end all ghost stories."

"Did you battle the possessed mannequin of a mortal enemy?" Kai guessed.

"Who tried to send you to the Departed Realm with magic blades?" Nya asked.

"But you defeated him first," Zane continued.

"And his ghost disappeared into the night," Lloyd said.

"So . . . yeah," Jay said, shrugging. "Why were all those ghosts out there?"

"Because distracting you was part of Master Yang's plan," Wu explained.

Morro floated over. "And Yang had help!"

When they saw Morro, the ninja all drew their weapons.

"Put away your weapons," Wu said. "Morro is here to help."

"Yang tricked Cole into helping him open a rift to return to the world," Morro explained.

The ninja looked around for Cole. Then they realized something: Cole wasn't there, and none of them had even noticed.

As the ninja and Wu raced to find their friend, Cole continued the fight against Master Yang.

"Just give up already," Yang told him.

"No!" screamed Cole. "I'm keeping you here until the eclipse ends and the rift closes. Your evil will never return."

Yang held up his Yin Blade. "What are you even fighting for? Your friends have abandoned you. Your Master has abandoned you. You are all alone!"

SETTLING A DEBT

Cole looked down at his hands. "I'm . . . fading away," he said sadly.

"Just one more lonely ghost," Yang laughed. "Not a friend in the world."

Just then, Cole heard a familiar voice.

"Cole!" It was Nya!

Cole spotted the *Destiny's Bounty* soaring through the sky. "My friends!"

At that moment, Cole's strength returned. He knocked Yang to the ground. "Ghost or not, I'm gonna do what I came here to do, Yang!

"You were wrong, Yang," Cole told him. "I'm not the one who's alone. You are!"

"No," Yang snapped, pointing to his students. "I have my family."

"No, you have prisoners. That's not family; that's captivity!" Cole said. Suddenly, his arms began to tingle. "I feel different . . . like I can punch through anything!" Cole cried, aiming another blow at Yang. The spell was broken.

"No!" Yang cried. One by one, his students shook off the spell that trapped them inside the temple.

"The rift!" Cole called to the students. "If you hurry, you can go through it and be free of this place forever!"

"I failed . . ." Yang moaned. "I always fail. I wanted to live forever, because I knew the day I was gone, no one would remember me."

"All of this was so you wouldn't be forgotten?" Cole asked him. "I get it. Believe me, I get it. I know what it's like to feel forgotten. It . . . hurts. But Master Yang, you *are* going to be remembered forever. You created Airjitzu!"

"Cole!" Kai screamed. "The rift! You gotta pass through the rift."

If Cole didn't go through the Rift of Return before it closed, he would remain a ghost forever.

"Come on," Cole said to Yang. "There's still time to go through. Both of us."

But Yang stopped. "The curse of the temple requires that at least one ghost remain behind as Master of the House." He grabbed Cole.

"What are you doing?" Cole screamed.

Master Yang smiled and threw him at the rift.

"Settling my debt."

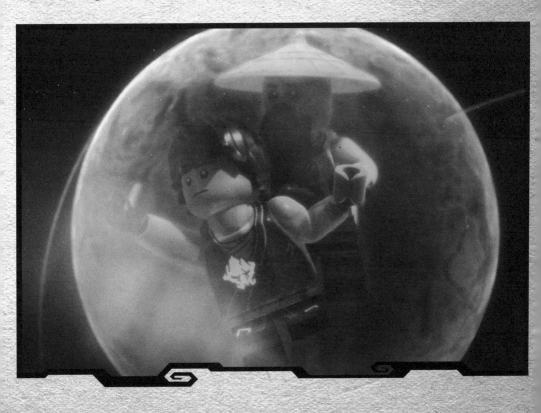

"Oh, no!" Jay wailed. "Cole is gone forever. I'd give anything to have him back."

"Anything?" Cole asked, stepping forward.

"Cole!" the ninja cried, running to hug their friend.

"You're not a ghost anymore," Lloyd said.

It was true. It had worked! Cole was human again.

"You look as good as new," Nya said.

"Thanks, Nya," Cole said, smiling at his friends. It was so good to be back with the team.